Library of Congress Cataloging-in-Publication Data

Szekeres, Cyndy.
    The mouse that Jack built / written and illustrated by Cyndy Szekeres.
        p. cm.
    Summary: Jack the bunny builds a wonderful snowmouse, decorating it with his own ragged hat and scarf, which he is able to leave on the snowmouse when his mother surprises him with a new hat and scarf.
    ISBN 0-590-69197-X
    [1. Snow — Fiction. 2. Snow sculpture — Fiction. 3. Clothing and dress — Fiction. 4. Rabbits — Fiction. 5. Stories in rhyme.]
    I. Title.
PZ8.3.S998Mo 1997
[E] — dc21   96-48182
                                                                                                         CIP
                                                                                                          AC

10 9 8 7 6 5 4 3 2 1
Printed in Singapore   46
First printing, November 1997

The Mouse That Jack Built

Written and Illustrated by

CYNDY SZEKERES

Cartwheel
B·O·O·K·S ® SCHOLASTIC INC.

New York Toronto London Auckland Sydney

For Emmett

This is the mouse that Jack built.

This is the raisin,
used for the nose,

on the face of the mouse that Jack built.

These are the whiskers
that wiggled and twitched,
causing poor Jack
to giggle and itch,
put next to the raisin,
used for the nose,
on the face of the mouse that Jack built.

Jack used his hat,
all ragged and worn,

along with his scarf,
all tattered and torn.

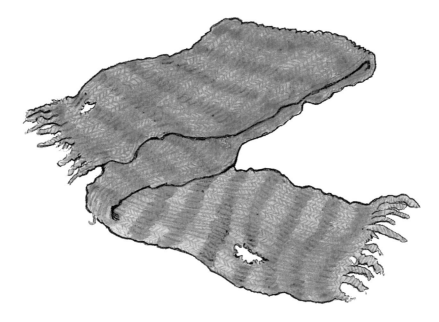

One sat on the head,
one wrapped 'round the neck,
brushed free of snowflakes,
every speck,
below the whiskers
that wiggled and twitched,
causing poor Jack
to giggle and itch,
put next to the raisin,
used for the nose,
on the face of the mouse that Jack built.

Mama called him with a scold,

"Jack, come home,
your supper's cold."

"Now, wear your hat,
though it's ragged and worn."

She put on his scarf,
all tattered and torn.

One had sat on the head,
one had wrapped 'round the neck,
brushed free of snowflakes,
every speck,
below the whiskers
that wiggled and twitched,
causing poor Jack
to giggle and itch,
put next to the raisin,
used for the nose,
on the face of the mouse that Jack built.

This is Jack.

He went home,

ate his supper,

and went to bed.

Early the next day...

Mama finished a new scarf and hat!
She sent Jack out
with a hug and a pat,

with his old hat,
all ragged and worn,
and that old scarf,
all tattered and torn,
to put back on

the mouse that Jack built!